nickelodeon™

5-Minute Christmas Stories Collection

Random House 🏠 New York

CONTENTS

The Pups Save Christmas!

Adapted from the teleplay by Ursula Ziegler Sullivan

Illustrated by Harry Moore

It was the day before Christmas. The PAW Patrol pups were excited to decorate the big pine tree outside the Lookout.

"I've got the popcorn!" Ryder announced as he walked out to the tree.

Rubble ran alongside him. "Hooray! A Christmas Eve snack!"

"This isn't for eating," Ryder said. "It's for hanging on the tree."

"Okay," Rubble replied. "My eyes will like seeing popcorn on the tree, but my tummy would rather eat it."

Everyone worked together. Ryder strung his popcorn along the branches, and Rocky hung lights. Marshall raised his fire truck ladder so he could put ornaments on the highest branches.

"I love Christmas," Zuma said with a sigh. "I can't wait for Santa to get here."

But Santa was flying into a blizzard! The storm rocked Santa's sleigh back and forth. Bags of presents fell out of it, and a big golden star slid off the front.

Santa guided the reindeer as the sleigh dipped sharply and landed hard in the snow.

Back at the Lookout, Ryder received a call on his PupPad. It was Santa Claus!

"My sleigh crashed, and I lost a load of gifts," he said. "My reindeer are lost now, too—and worst of all, my Magic Christmas Star is gone! That's what gives my sleigh and reindeer the power to fly! Without it, I'll never finish delivering my gifts."

"We'll do everything we can to help, Santa!" said Ryder.

Ryder told the pups about Santa's problems.

"Rubble, I need your shovel to dig the sleigh out of the snow."

"Rubble on the double!" Rubble shouted.

Ryder looked at Rocky. "I need your forklift to help raise Santa's sleigh out of the snow, and some recycled parts to fix it."

"Don't lose it—reuse it!" said Rocky.

"Skye, Zuma, and Marshall," Ryder continued, "I need your helicopter, hovercraft, and fire truck to help find the loads of presents Santa lost."

"This pup's got to fly!" Skye exclaimed.

"Let's dive in!" Zuma cheered.

"I'm fired up!" Marshall declared.

"And, Chase," Ryder said, "I need you to round up Santa's reindeer."

"Chase is on the case!" he shouted.

"All right! The PAW Patrol is ready to roll!" Ryder exclaimed,
and all the pups raced away from the Lookout.

Ryder and Rocky found Santa's sleigh! Rocky lifted it with his truck.

"The crash broke off one of the runners," Ryder said. "We'll have to replace it, Rocky."

"This storm is getting worse," said Rocky. "We'd better get it fixed in a hurry!"

Skye zoomed through the blustery night, looking for the lost bags of presents. Her searchlight scanned the dark forest.

"I see a bag," she reported to Ryder.

Chase and Marshall found another bag in the high branches, so Marshall extended his ladder to reach it. He carefully climbed to the top—and slipped off the ladder!

The bag tumbled down behind him.

Chase quickly launched
a net to catch the falling bag
of gifts. Marshall landed
in the soft snow.

"I'm good," he announced
with a smile.

Skye, Chase, and Marshall found the other bags of gifts and met Ryder at the sleigh. They got there just as Rocky started to attach an old ski to the bottom of the sleigh.

"I knew this would come in handy," he said proudly.

"It's got to be here somewhere," Ryder said as he, Rocky, and Rubble searched outside Farmer Yumi's barn for the Magic Christmas Star.

Rocky heard Bettina, Farmer Yumi's cow, mooing. "Maybe Bettina saw it. Hey, where is she?"

They glanced around, but no one saw her . . . until Ryder pointed up at the night sky.

Ryder and the pups couldn't believe their eyes. Bettina was flying through the air—with the Christmas star stuck to her side!

"The star is making her fly like a reindeer!" Ryder exclaimed.

"How will we get her down?" Rocky asked.

Ryder grabbed some hay and whistled to Bettina. "Fresh hay! Come and get it!"

Bettina floated down for her snack. While she was munching the hay, Rocky used a mechanical claw from his Pup Pack to grab the Magic Christmas Star.

Meanwhile, Chase had found all eight of the reindeer, but they wouldn't line up. He decided this was a job for his loudspeaker. "ATTENTION, ALL REINDEER!" he announced. "Please move forward in an orderly fashion!"

They did as they were told, and Chase led them back to Santa's sleigh.

When Ryder and the pups met at the sleigh, they found
Santa Claus waiting for them.

"My sleigh looks perfect!" he exclaimed.

"Except for one missing piece," Ryder said, holding
out the Magic Christmas Star. Santa took it and hung it
on the front of the sleigh.

"I don't know how to thank you, Ryder," Santa said.
"I thought Christmas would be ruined, but you and the
pups saved it!"

Shimmer and Shine™

Santa's Christmas Genies

Adapted by Hollis James from the teleplay "My Secret Genies"
by Sindy Boveda Spackman

Illustrated by Mattia Francesco Laviosa

It was the day before Christmas, and Leah had almost finished writing her letter to Santa when her neighbor Zac knocked at the door. He needed stamps for his own letter to Santa.

"All I want for Christmas is a canoe," he said.

"I'm asking Santa for snow on Christmas," Leah said, holding up her snowflake-shaped letter.

Zac wanted to get home to make room for his canoe, so Leah offered to mail his letter to Santa for him.

Leah called for Shimmer and Shine, and they appeared in a *poof* of sparkles with their pets, Tala and Nahal.

Shimmer and Shine didn't know what Christmas was, so Leah explained it to them.

"First you write a letter to Santa about what you want for Christmas. Then Santa's elves make the presents in his workshop for Santa to deliver by Christmas morning!"

The genies were happy to help Leah.

"Boom, Zahramay!" Shimmer chanted.

"First wish of the day! Shimmer and Shine, get this letter to Santa divine!"

Suddenly, Leah and the genies, along with Tala and
Nahal, were standing in the snowy North Pole.
"I just wanted to get the letter to Santa," Leah said.
"I didn't think I'd be giving it to him in person!"
"Oh, snowball!" said Shimmer. "My mistake, Leah."
"This mistake is great!" exclaimed Leah. "Because
now I get to meet Santa!"

Leah gave Zac's letter to Santa. But Santa already knew about the canoe. "Zac's been sending me a letter every day since last Christmas!" he said, chuckling.

Santa gave Leah and the genies a tour of his workshop. They saw busy elves making toys, and the reindeer who pulled his sleigh.

At the end of the tour, Santa said, "I hope you enjoyed visiting my workshop."

"We did," said Leah, shivering. "I wish you lived someplace warmer, though."

"Boom, Zahramay! Second wish of the day!" Shine chanted. "Shimmer and Shine, get Santa someplace warmer divine!"

Whoosh! Santa was whisked away to a tropical island.

"I didn't mean to make *that* wish!" cried Leah. "Not when Santa still has presents to deliver."

"Oh, right," said Shine. "I forgot about that part. My mistake."

When the elves heard that Santa was gone, they started to panic.

"I wish these elves would calm down!" said Leah.

"*Boom, Zahramay, third wish of the day!*" Shimmer sang. "*Shimmer and Shine, elves calm down divine!*"

With those words, the elves fell into a deep sleep.

"That was my last wish!" exclaimed Leah. "We need those elves to be awake so they can finish the presents."

"Oh, sleigh bells," cried Shimmer. "My mistake, Leah. I thought that's what you wished for."

"I did," replied Leah. "So it was *my* mistake. Maybe it'll be all right—as long as we finish these presents and find Santa!"

The gifts were loaded onto Santa's sleigh. It was time to make the deliveries, but the genies weren't sure where to go.

"Maybe we should press this button with the picture of Santa on it!" said Shine.

"Don't press the button," warned Leah and Shimmer.

But Shine couldn't help herself. "I'm pressing the button!"

Shine had pressed the Santa-tracking button. The reindeer leapt into the air and flew Leah and her friends right to the beach where Santa was stranded.

The sleigh crashed to a stop in the sand. Leah and her friends tried to get the sleigh out, but it was stuck.

"If only we had something else that Santa could fly," said Leah.

"How about a magic carpet?" suggested Shimmer.

Together the sisters chanted: *"Shimmer and Shine, double genie magic divine!"*

Poof! Santa was back in his red suit and perched on a magic carpet.

"Ho, ho, ho!" he exclaimed. "It's time to save Christmas!"

Flying from house to house, Leah, Shimmer, and Shine helped Santa deliver presents all around the world.

Shimmer and Shine flew away on their magic carpet.
As they sailed out of sight, they sang:
"*We saved the day with three merry wishes! Boom, Zahramay!*
We'll see you next Christmas!"

Happy Holidays, Bubble Guppies!

Adapted by Mary Tillworth
Based on the teleplay "Happy Holidays, Mr. Grumpfish!"
by Adam Peltzman

Illustrated by MJ Illustrations

Hi! It's me, Molly. It's a special time of year. The snow is on the ground, and the decorations are on the houses. And the best part is that we're having a holiday party tonight. It's going to be *fin*-tastic!

But we have a lot to do first—like bake treats and deliver invitations. Gil and Bubble people are ready to help. Will you join us?

We're inviting everyone in town, and we've delivered almost all of the invitations. There's only one left. It's for . . . Mr. Grumpfish. That sad blue house is his. He never seems very happy and doesn't seem to like anyone. Maybe getting a card will make him happy. He might like to come to our holiday party. Do you think we can find a way to cheer him up?

It's time to help Deema bake gingerbread cookies for the party. She's a great baker, but she has to make a lot of cookies and can't do it all herself. We'll help measure, mix, and decorate. I love all the shapes and colors, but the best part is the smell!

All this delicious gingerbread gives me an idea. I think I know something that might make Mr. Grumpfish happy. But it's going to take a lot of work, so we better get moving!

For my special project we needs lots of marshmallow frosting, so we're at Marshmallow Mountain. But we have to watch out for the Abominable Snowman. He doesn't like to share his gooey frosting.

However, the Abominable Snowman also doesn't like it when people don't enjoy the holidays. He let us take all the frosting we need to make Mr. Grumpfish happy.

Now we're ready to make our special surprise. We're going to turn Mr. Grumpfish's sad blue house into a giant gingerbread house! With a little help from Nonny the candy-cane maker, we have everything we need. Everyone is pitching in and carrying gumballs and bows. Even Mr. Grouper is helping us decorate.

The house is done and looks delicious.
We hope Mr. Grumpfish likes it and
comes to our holiday party.

When Mr. Grumpfish came out of his house he saw the frosting and candy and gingerbread. It made him giggle a little, then belly-laugh a lot. He loved his sweet, festive house.

Mr. Grumpfish was so happy, he couldn't wait to get to the party. And when he was there, Mr. Grouper let him turn on the Christmas tree lights!

The holiday party is great! Everyone agrees it's the best one ever! And though we all really like giving and getting gifts, the thing we love best is being together. It's especially nice because our new friend Mr. Grumpfish is with us!

At the end of the party, we all gather around the Christmas tree for a picture. Say "Gingerbread!"

That's the end of our party and our adventure. Gil and I are so glad you could join us. Happy holidays!

Santa's Little Helpers

Based on the teleplay "Santa's Little Fixers"
by P. Kevin Strader and Jennifer Twomey

Illustrated by Bob Ostrom

Do you see
a star?

It was Christmas Eve. The stockings were hung, and the tree was decorated. Team Umizoomi was ready for Santa to visit.

"I can't wait to see what Santa brings," Milli said.

Suddenly, the Umi Alarm rang. Someone needed help!

Bot had a message on his Belly, Belly, Bellyscreen. It was from Santa Claus!

"Help, Team Umizoomi!" Santa said. "My toy machine stopped working, and we still need to make three more toys!"

"If the machine isn't fixed," Bot said, "Santa won't be able to deliver all the toys tonight!"

"We need to get to the North Pole and help Santa," Geo said.

"The best way to get to the North Pole is on a reindeer," said Geo. "I can make one with my Super Shapes! We need five triangles, one trapezoid, and antlers. *Super Shapes!*"

"*Glittering Gizmos!*" Bot shouted as Team Umizoomi flew through the air on their reindeer. It got colder and colder. Snow started to fall.

At last, they landed at the North Pole.
"Look!" said Milli. "There's Santa's workshop!"

How many
candy canes
do you see?

Santa welcomed Team Umizoomi into his workshop. "Thank goodness you're here," he said. "The toy machine is broken, and we still have to make a sailboat, a dollhouse, and a fire truck."

"Don't worry, Santa," Geo said. "We'll fix this machine with our Mighty Math Powers!" Then he and the rest of the team climbed into the machine.

"To fix the machine," Bot said, "we have to know how it works. Let's check my Super Robot Computer."

The computer told Team Umizoomi that the first section of the machine was filled with buckets carrying toy parts. The next section was the Magic Duster, where the parts were put together. The last section wrapped the toys.

"Let's fix this machine!" said Geo.

Team Umizoomi found the part of the machine with the buckets. The conveyor belts were stuck, and the gears weren't turning. Geo looked at the buckets. "First, we have to find the buckets with the parts for a sailboat, a dollhouse, and a fire truck."

How many green buckets do you see?

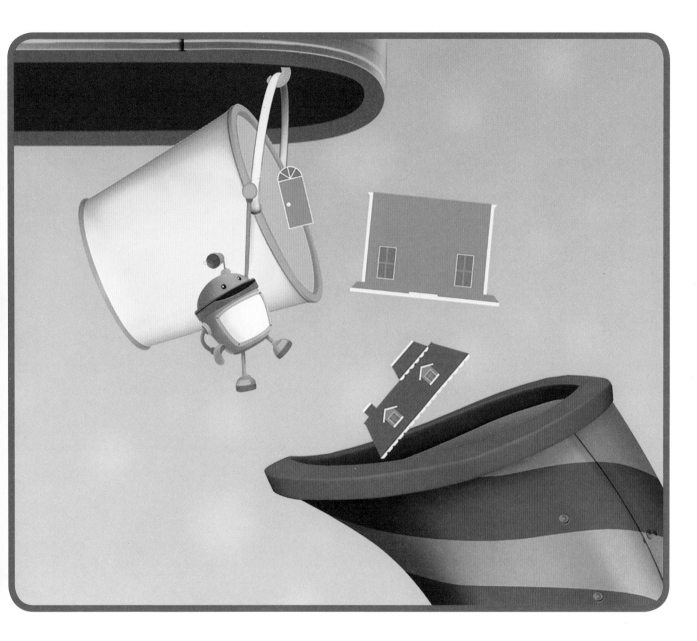

Team Umizoomi looked and looked—and they found the parts! Bot emptied them into a tube that was striped like a candy cane, and the machine started to work again.

"Now let's find the Magic Duster," Milli said.

The team quickly found the Magic Duster, but none of Santa's magic dust was coming out.

"We have to fix the Duster," Bot said, "or the last three toys won't get made."

"Look!" Milli shouted. "Those instruments play a special song that makes the dust come out. But one of the instruments is missing! I can fix this with *Pattern Power*!"

"The instruments are supposed to make the pattern jingle bell, trumpet, trumpet. Let's see which one is missing." Milli studied the machine. "A jingle bell!"

Milli replaced the missing bell, and the machine started puffing magic dust that put the toys together!

The sailboat, the dollhouse, and the fire truck were finished, and they rolled into the Wrapper. Robot hands wrapped them in brightly colored paper.

"Hooray, Team Umizoomi!" Santa's elves cheered. "You did it! You made the last three presents."

"Let's get these presents to Santa," said Geo.

Team Umizoomi ran to Santa's sleigh and put the last three presents in his sack.

"Thank you!" Santa said. Then, as his sleigh flew into the starry night, he called out, "Merry Christmas!"

"I feel a celebration coming on!" Bot announced. Team Umizoomi and the elves danced in the snow and cheered.

ALBERT

The Little Tree with Big Dreams

By Aaron and Will Eisenberg

Illustrated by Heather Martinez

No one loved Christmastime more than the plants at Earth Mama's nursery. Holiday cheer seeped through their roots. Maisie the palm tree swayed in her pot, and even Gene the stink-breath weed got in on the fun!

Little Albert was about to bring them more joy with a Christmas song.

"Who's ready to get their jingle on?" Albert called. "This is gonna be the Christmas-iest Christmas of all!"

But every year, as Albert watched all the big trees outside go home with happy families, he grew a little sad.

"Look at those guys," Albert sighed. "They're going to get shiny stars, and on Christmas morning, kids will go crazypants for the presents under their branches."

Albert loved his nursery family, but he knew he was destined for something greater.

Albert slumped in his pot . . . until a man on TV caught his attention.

"Tomorrow in Baker's Hill, Vermont," the man explained, "one special tree, oozing with Christmas spirit, will be chosen as this year's Empire City Christmas Tree— the most famous Christmas tree in the world!"

A special tree, oozing with Christmas spirit? That sounded like Albert! He decided to do something big. He would sneak a ride to Baker's Hill with the girl and her dad.

Gene thought Albert was out of his mulch.

But Maisie believed in him. She wanted to come along!

The second the coast was clear, Albert and his buddies snuck out to Donny's truck to stow away in the back. Donny had a plant delivery at Baker's Hill before the Empire City Christmas Show in New York.

Maisie bent her trunk backward and launched Albert and Gene into the truck, then jumped in behind them.

They waved goodbye to their Earth Mama's family and set off.

Soon Molly and Donny stopped for lunch at a restaurant called Cactus Pete's.

"Help!" a voice called from beneath the snow. Albert got out of the truck and started digging. He was surprised to find Cactus Pete himself!

The freezing cactus groaned. "E-e-every winter I'm tossed out so some s-s-stinkin' Christmas tree can take my place inside."

Maisie perked up. "Did you say Christmas tree? Albert here is going to be the Empire City Christmas Tree!"

"Oh, is he?" sneered Pete, sharpening his needles.

"Well, considerin' I *hate* Christmas," he howled, "allow Cactus Pete to show y'all a prickly good time!"

Pete and his ragtag band of cacti chased after Albert, Maisie, and Gene, blasting spiky needles in every direction! Many of Albert's ornaments fell to the ground and shattered.

But Albert and his friends bested the cacti and rolled a dumpster right at Cactus Pete, flattening him like a pancake.

The plants escaped and headed into a nearby forest in search of Baker's Hill. There they came across a family of rabbits. "Aww! Fuzzy widdle bunnies!" Maisie gushed. CHOMP! A rabbit took a giant bite out of her leaves. "It's a vegetarian!" yelled Gene. "Run!"

They all jumped onto a log and slid down an enormous hill.

At last, they were there! Empire City Square. The purple sky swirled into the stinging December wind. Maisie's teeth chattered!

A massive crowd gathered around Big Betty, the eighty-foot evergreen, ready to ring in the season.

Albert, Maisie, and Gene spotted Cactus Pete. He was aiming a spike right at the crane operator who was about to put the famous star on Betty's head.

"Look," Pete cackled. "A fallin' star!"

POP! WHIZ! SHING! Pete's needles pierced the operator right in the heinie, sending the star swinging above. It sliced Betty's top clean off!

"I'm bald!" Betty cried.

There was no place to put the famous star! Christmas was ruined.

Albert looked out at the heartbroken crowd. Right in the middle, he saw Molly, the girl from the nursery! He remembered something she had once told him: *"It's okay to be small, as long as it doesn't stop you from doin' big things."*

Albert had an idea! But he needed help.

People in the crowd gave Albert some new decorations, and the crane operator hoisted him up. And up!

And up.

Cameras flashed and the crowd
cheered as Albert was lifted onto Betty's
peak and the spectacular star was placed
on top of his head. At three feet tall,
he was a perfect fit!

Albert had done it! He had become the most famous Christmas tree in the world! But when he looked down at Maisie and Gene waving goodbye, he realized something was missing: his family at Earth Mama's nursery. Christmastime just didn't feel like Christmastime without them.

Then Albert saw Cactus Pete. He was sad and alone.
"You don't hate Christmas," Albert said. An idea was sparking inside him. "You just hate being left out. How'd you like to be shiny and twinkly for once?"

Albert traded places with the cactus. Pete immediately started singing at the top of his lungs. *"O Cactus Pete! O Cactus Pete! How heavenly are thy needles!"*

Big Betty rolled her eyes. "This is gonna be one long holiday."

Albert, Maisie, and Gene looked at Pete and smiled. It was time to go home.

On Christmas morning, Molly stuck a tiny star on Albert's tip.
"Every real Christmas tree needs a star," she said.
Albert smiled. It was going to be the Christmas-iest Christmas
after all!

The Sponge Who Saved
CHRISTMAS

Written by Melissa Wygand

Illustrated by Fabrizio Petrossi

It was Christmastime in Bikini Bottom. Decorations were being hung. Gifts were being wrapped. Everyone loved the holiday season. Well, almost everyone.

Squidward didn't like Christmas
because at that time of year, SpongeBob
was even happier and more annoying
than usual!

SpongeBob decided to share as much seasonal
joy with Squidward as possible. So whenever he
and Patrick had a snowball fight, they made sure to
include Squidward—whether he was ready or not.

SpongeBob and Patrick tried to lift Squidward's spirits by singing Christmas carols all day long. Everywhere Squidward went, they shared the gift of music with him. But that didn't seem to work, either.

"I've had enough of this holiday!" yelled Squidward. "It's all Santa this, and presents that!

"And who does this Santa guy think he is, anyway? He's got a flying sleigh and magic reindeer? He gives you stuff for free? I'll believe it when I see it!"

"If Santa's as great as everyone says he is,"
Squidward demanded, "then why can't he shovel
my snow?"

SpongeBob didn't have an answer. He sadly walked home.

Squidward didn't hear anything from SpongeBob for the rest of the day. He settled into his bed that night, pleased at the idea that Christmas would be over soon and things would be back to normal. But just as he was falling asleep, bright lights filled the room.

Squidward ran to the window. "You've got to be kidding me!" he exclaimed.

Across the way, SpongeBob's house was covered with colorful flashing and blinking lights and other Christmas decorations!

WELCOME

HI

SANTA!

HI

HI

Squidward marched over to SpongeBob's house and took all his Christmas lights down. Then he snuck inside and took down all his decorations, too!

But just as Squidward was finishing up, SpongeBob came out of his bedroom. In the dark, SpongeBob thought he was looking at Santa Claus. Squidward didn't want to get caught, so he played along.

"Could you please take this present to my friend Squidward Tentacles?" SpongeBob said.

Squidward was very surprised. He promised he would deliver the present. Then SpongeBob gave Squidward a big hug and went back to bed.

Curious, Squidward quickly tore open the wrapping paper. Inside was a beautifully crafted clarinet case made of the best driftwood money could buy!

Then Squidward realized what Christmas was all about. It wasn't just about snowball fights, caroling, or even big flashy lights. It was also about friends, and being kind to them.

And so, one by one, Squidward returned all of
SpongeBob's lights and decorations to their proper
spots. The house was lit up once again.

"It's going to be a merry Christmas after all," Squidward said.

Adapted by Frank Berrios
Based on the teleplay "Blaze Christmas"
by Jeff Borkin

Illustrated by Dynamo Limited

'Twas the night before Christmas,
and all through Axle City,
big-wheeled Monster Machines
were making their homes look pretty.

Stripes put a wreath on his tree house,
and Starla decorated her barn.
Zeg got ready for Christmas
with ornaments, tinsel, and yarn.

Darington was so excited,
he jumped to his highest height!
Everyone knew they'd be getting a visit
from Santa tonight!

Meanwhile, Blaze and AJ
were far, far away,
helping Santa get ready
for another Christmas Day!

Blaze raced around the workshop as elf trucks tossed presents into Santa's magic bag.

"Santa's bag can hold presents for everyone in the world!" said AJ.

"My elves and I make sure we've got the perfect present for every boy and girl," said Santa. "Everyone should feel special on Christmas!"

"The present meter says the bag is full!" exclaimed Blaze.

"Ho, ho, ho! Now I've got Christmas presents for everyone!" chuckled Santa Claus.

Santa and his friends were so busy that no one noticed two uninvited guests.

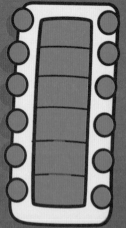

"Hey, Crusher, what are we doing in Santa's workshop?" asked Pickle.

"I want to look in Santa's bag and find my Christmas present," whispered Crusher. But before he could find his present, the bag began to roll away . . . with Crusher on top of it!

"Oh, no! The Christmas presents are getting away!" yelled an elf truck.

"Quick, after them!" said Blaze. He, AJ, and Santa raced after Crusher and the presents!

The bag rolled down a hill. It spilled open, and presents soared through the air in every direction!

"My magic bag is empty. Now I can't deliver my presents to anyone," Santa said sadly.

"Don't worry, Santa," said AJ. "Those presents are out there somewhere."

"And AJ and I are going to find them!" added Blaze.

"Wait—I want to come, too," begged Crusher.

"Good for you, Crusher! You feel bad, and now you want to help get all the presents back," said Pickle.

"*All* the presents? No way. I just want to get *my* present back," replied Crusher.

"Remember, Crusher, it's important that you help Blaze find *everyone's* present," said Santa. "Everyone should feel special on Christmas."

Blaze and Crusher raced into a frosty cave where they found some of the presents frozen in ice. Crusher tried to use a suction-cup bow and arrow to get them, but it couldn't fly far enough.

Then Blaze had an idea. "Let's be engineers and build a *better* bow and arrow!"

Together they made a giant bendy bow with a big suction cup to attach to the presents. AJ aimed, hit the mark, and pulled the presents from the ice. Unfortunately, none of the gifts were Crusher's. The trio kept searching.

Blaze and Crusher rushed off to search. Soon they spotted a pile of presents at the bottom of a very steep hill covered in candy canes!

"We have to make a sled that goes really fast!" said AJ. "Let's build a sled with a turbojet engine!"

"Woo-hoo! I'm a turbo-sled Monster Machine!" said Blaze. He took off with a burst down the candy-cane cliff and used his tow hook to snag the presents. Blaze added them to Santa's bag.

"Look! The red line on Santa's bag is going up!" noticed AJ. "That means we've found almost all the Christmas presents."

Crusher peered into the bag. "All these presents, and none of them are for me!" he whined.

The group continued.

They came to Snowball Mountain, which was shooting giant snowballs!

To stop the snowballs, Blaze transformed into a big water blaster.

"Oh, yeah! I'm a water-blastin' Monster Machine!" he shouted. "Time to get those Christmas presents."

When the Monster Machines reached the top of the mountain, Crusher found what he was looking for.

"I got my present!" he sang. But while the big blue truck celebrated, the ice on the mountaintop began to give way!

"Oh, no! Santa's bag is falling!" cried AJ.

"It's too heavy," said Blaze. "I can't pull it up by myself."

"Well, good luck with that!" Crusher said. "I've already got my present." The present made him feel special. But then Crusher remembered what Santa had said: *everyone* should feel special on Christmas. "If those presents fall, no one will get a present from Santa. And then no one will feel special on Christmas! I've got to save those presents!"

Crusher went back to Blaze. Using their tow hooks, Blaze and Crusher worked together to save the Christmas presents.

Santa was so grateful to the Monster Machines, he told
Blaze he could be his sleigh.

And so it was, with Blaze as the sleigh,
Santa's gifts were delivered for Christmas Day.
And as they flew out of sight, we heard a phrase:
"Merry Christmas to all! And to all a 'Let's blaaaze!'"

Dora's Christmas Star

Adapted by Mary Tillworth
Based on the teleplay "Dora's Christmas Carol Adventure"
by Chris Gifford

Illustrated by Victoria Miller

One beautiful Christmas Eve, Dora and her friends came together under a starry sky. They were excited because it was time for their special *Nochebuena* party. Soon there would be gifts and games and tasty treats, but first they had to get ready. Everyone happily worked together to make the party the best it could be.

"It's my favorite night of the year!" said Dora. "I love to wear my holiday dress, decorate the tree, and celebrate with all my friends."

Because it was such a special night, everyone had worn their very best for the party. Dora twirled in her pretty dress. Her friends all oohed and aahed.

Boots, dressed in his nicest holiday sweater, proudly adjusted his fancy purple bow tie. Isa wore her favorite dress—and her shiniest necklace!

"Let's decorate the tree!" said Dora.

The friends all helped each other and sang Christmas carols while they trimmed the tree. Boots hung shiny ornaments on the branches. Isa strung twinkling lights. Tico and Benny wrapped the tree in glittering garlands. The tree was beautiful, but it was missing one important piece.

Finally, Dora placed a shiny star at the very top.

"Our Christmas tree looks *perfecto*!" she exclaimed.

At last it was time for the most exciting
part of the night: the gifts!
"Christmas is a time for giving," said Isa.
Dora and all her friends agreed.

Dora, Boots, and their friends worked together to carefully place the Christmas presents under the tree. The colorful wrapping paper glittered as the presents piled up.

Just then, Swiper appeared. He saw the pretty star on top of the tree, climbed up, and swiped it! "You'll never find it now!" he said, laughing as he threw it high into the air.

Suddenly, someone swooped down from the sky. It was Santa! He wanted to surprise everyone by coming to Dora's *Nochebuena* party.

When Santa saw that the star was missing from the tree,
he knew Swiper had swiped it.

"Swiper, I've told you before, and now I must insist.
Swiping on Christmas puts you on my Naughty List," said
Santa.

Dora and her friends knew what that meant. If Swiper
was on the Naughty List, he wouldn't get any presents, and
he would have a very sad Christmas!

"Santa, is there anything we can do to get Swiper off the
Naughty List?" Dora asked. "I really want to help him."

Santa thought for a moment. "If Swiper can learn the true
meaning of Christmas, I will change my mind," he said.

"Remember what Christmas is all about," Dora told Swiper. Swiper thought for a moment. "Christmas is about sharing and giving—not swiping," he said. He quickly found the star ornament high up in a tree and gave it back to Dora.

"Ho, ho, ho!" laughed Santa. "Swiper, you have learned the true meaning of Christmas. You are officially on my Nice List!"

It was time for the *Nochebuena* party! Benny brought tasty nuts for Tico. The Big Red Chicken brought Christmas cookies for Benny. Isa brought colorful flowers for everyone.

Dora and her friends ate *caramelos* and drank hot chocolate and danced and celebrated.

"This is the best *Nochebuena* party ever!" said Dora.

Finally, it was time to go home. Everyone had had a great time at the *Nochebuena* party.

Before he left, Santa gave everyone a hug—even Swiper, who had been a very good fox after all. Then Santa climbed into his sleigh, shook the reins, and flew into the sky. He waved goodbye as the sleigh zoomed away.

"I'm so glad I got to celebrate Christmas Eve with all my friends," said Dora.

"Merry Christmas! *¡Feliz Navidad!*"

Save the Reindeer!

Adapted by Tone Thyne

Based on the teleplay written by Chris Nee

Illustrated by Michael Scanlon,
Little Airplane Productions

It was Christmas Eve, and the Wonder Pets were happily singing and trimming the tree.

But while the Wonder Pets were singing, their tin-can phone started ringing. That meant an animal needed help!

"It's a reindeer!"
shouted Tuck. "She's on
the ice in the North Pole,
and she looks stuck."

"The North Pole!" Tuck exclaimed.
"She must be one of Santa's reindeer."

"This is as serious as it gets," said
Ming-Ming. "Let's go, Wonder Pets!"

"Let's save the reindeer!" the Wonder
Pets sang.

The Wonder Pets quickly assembled their Flyboat.
They put on the wheels and the mast. Then, for a
little bit of Christmas spirit, they added candy canes.

When the Christmas Flyboat was ready, they
jumped aboard and zoomed to the rescue.

They sailed through the night.
It got colder and colder. Soon the
North Pole was in sight.

"If we don't find the baby reindeer, Santa won't be able to deliver his presents," Linny said.

"But I can't live in a world without presents," cried Ming-Ming. The Wonder Pets realized they weren't just saving the reindeer—they were saving Christmas!

At last, they spotted the baby reindeer.

As the Wonder Pets flew closer, they could hear the ice cracking. They knew they had to act quickly. Luckily, they had an unopened present with them. Inside was a purple sweater that Tuck had knitted for Ming-Ming.

"Thank you," Ming-Ming said. "Purple really is my color."

The Wonder Pets used the sweater as a net to grab the baby reindeer. They flew in close and wrapped her in the sweater. Then they pulled her up together.

As they soared away, the ice cracked! They had saved the baby reindeer just in time!

The Wonder Pets brought the baby reindeer back to Santa's house. She thanked Linny, Tuck, and Ming-Ming, then joined the rest of the reindeer team.

Just then, Santa came out of his house. The Wonder Pets couldn't believe their eyes!

"What a wonderful night for flying," Santa said with a jolly laugh. He climbed into his sleigh, and the reindeer carried him into the sky. Christmas was saved!

It was getting late, but the Wonder Pets
knew they could still fly home in time for
their Christmas Eve fun. As they raced
through the sky, they sang.

'Wonder Pets! Wonder Pets! We found a way
to help the baby reindeer and save the day!
We're not too big, and we're not too tough.
But when we work together, we've got the right stuff!'

When they finally arrived home, they
made a wonderful discovery. . . .

Santa had already visited and left gifts for them. There was a special star on their tree, a beautiful snow globe, and best of all . . . celery!